PEACE AT LAST

PEACE AT LAST

by Jill Murphy

A Puffin Pied Piper

For
Daniel
Celia and
Min

Library of Congress Catalog Card Number: 80-66743
First Pied Piper Printing 1982
Printed in Hong Kong by South China Printing Co.
O B E
13 15 17 19 20 18 16 14
A Pied Piper Book is a registered trademark of
Dial Books for Young Readers,
A member of Penguin Putnam Inc.
® TM 1,163,686 and ® TM 1,054,312.
PEACE AT LAST is published in a hardcover edition by
Dial Books for Young Readers
375 Hudson Street, New York, New York 10014
ISBN 0-14-054685-5

The hour was late.

Mr. Bear was tired,
Mrs. Bear was tired,
and Baby Bear was tired,
so they all went to bed.

Mrs. Bear fell asleep.

Mr. Bear didn't.

Mrs. Bear began to snore.
"SNORE," went Mrs. Bear.
"SNORE, SNORE, SNORE."
"Oh, NO!" said Mr. Bear,
"I can't stand THIS."
So he got up and went to
sleep in Baby Bear's room.

 Baby Bear was not asleep either.
He was lying in bed, pretending
to be an airplane.
"NYAAOW!" went Baby Bear.
"NYAAOW! NYAAOW!"
"Oh, NO!" said Mr. Bear,
"I can't stand THIS."
So he got up
and went to sleep in the living room.

TICK-TOCK . . . went the living room
clock. . . .TICK-TOCK, TICK-TOCK,
CUCKOO! CUCKOO!
"Oh, NO!" said Mr. Bear,
"I can't stand THIS."
So he went off to sleep in the kitchen.

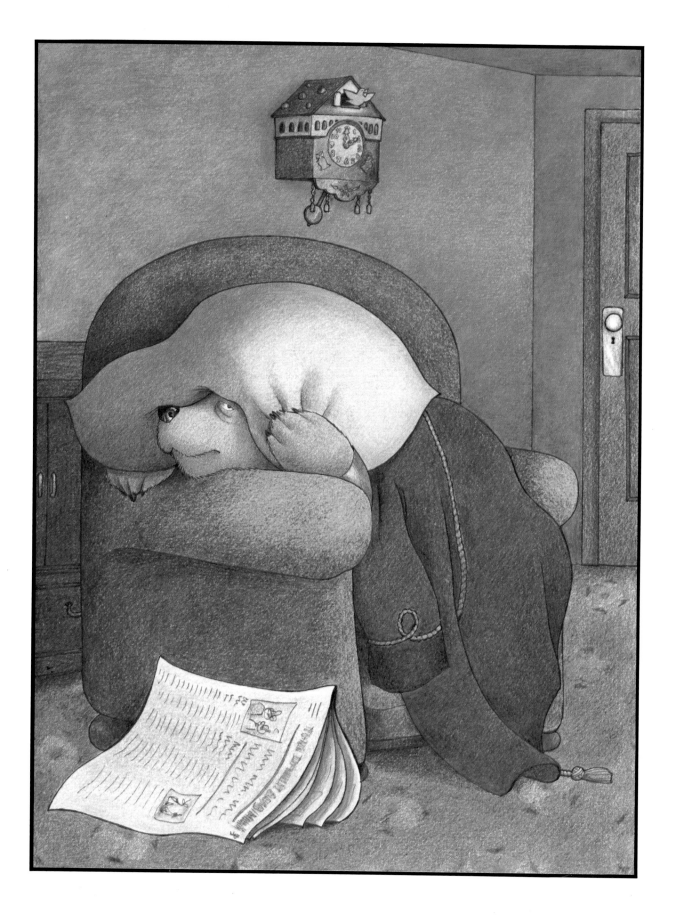

DRIP, DRIP . . . went the leaky
kitchen faucet.
HMMMMMMMMMM . . .
went the refrigerator.
"Oh, NO," said Mr. Bear,
"I can't stand THIS."
So he got up
and went to sleep in the garden.

Well, you would not believe
what noises there are in
the garden at night.
"TOO-WHIT-TOO-WHOO!"
went the owl.
"SNUFFLE, SNUFFLE," went
the hedgehog.
"MIAAAOW!" sang the cats
on the wall.
"Oh, NO!" said Mr. Bear,
"I can't stand THIS."
So he went off to sleep in
the car.

It was cold in the car
and uncomfortable, but
Mr. Bear was so tired
that he didn't notice.
He was just falling asleep
when all the birds started to
sing and the sun peeped in at
the window.
"TWEET TWEET!" went the birds.
SHINE, SHINE . . . went the sun.
"Oh, NO!" said Mr. Bear,
"I can't stand THIS."
So he got up and went back
into the house.

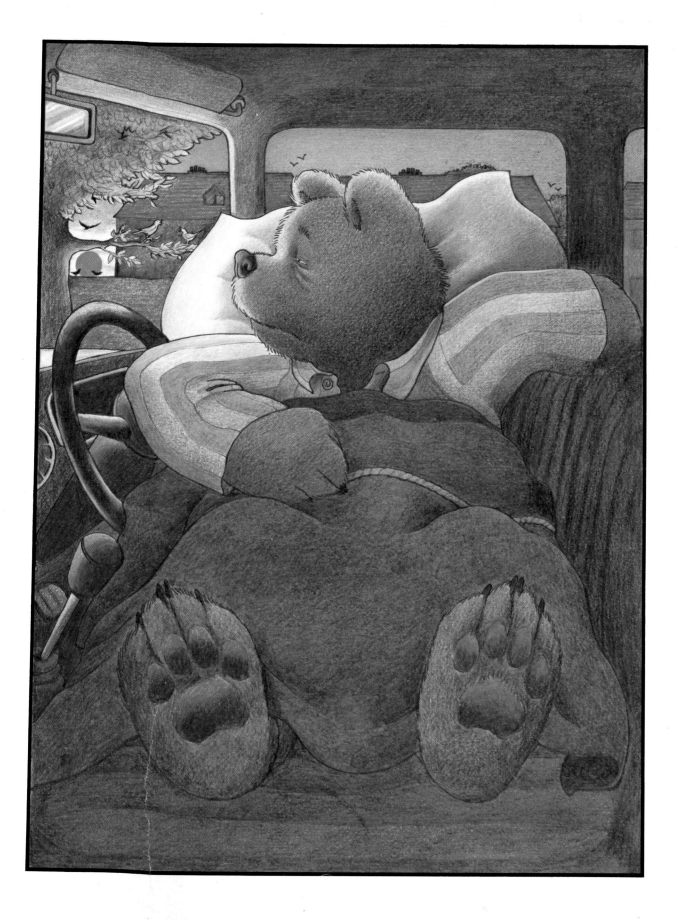

In the house Baby Bear was
fast asleep, and Mrs. Bear had
turned over and wasn't snoring
anymore.
Mr. Bear got into bed and closed his
eyes.
"Peace at last," he said to himself.

BRRRRRRRRRRRRRR . . . went the
alarm clock. BRRRRRR!
Mrs. Bear sat up and rubbed her eyes.
"Good morning, dear," she said.
"Did you sleep well?"
"Not VERY well, dear," yawned Mr. Bear.
"Never mind," said Mrs. Bear. "I'll
bring you the mail and a nice cup of tea."

And she did.

JILL MURPHY

was born and raised in London, where she has been writing and drawing since the age of three. She is the author-illustrator of two previous picture books, one of which was serialized on BBC-TV in Great Britain.